WAITING
FOR
THE
WESTBOUND
●

WAITING FOR THE WESTBOUND

Ruth Allison Coates

OCEAN TREE BOOKS

Also by Ruth Allison Coates:
GREAT AMERICAN NATURALISTS

My special thanks to these people—Richard Louis Polese, who first encouraged me to put this volume together, then guided it every step of the way; writer Cathy Lenox; and poet Judyth Hill, who, across the miles became a trusted friend and advisor.

"To Market, To Market" was first published in *Indiannual 3*.
"Now Are We Here" appeared first in *Indiana Writes*.

Copyright © 1992 Ruth Allison Coates
First Edition. Printed in U. S. A.

Published by:
OCEAN TREE BOOKS
Post Office Box 1295
Santa Fe, New Mexico 87504

Please write for our complete list of travel, peacemaking, poetry and inspirational titles.

Design: Richard Louis Polese
Typography: Pat Waganaar

International Standard Book Number 0-943734-18-5

Library of Congress CIP Catalog Number 92-13955

For my four children . . . and Robert

WAITING
FOR
THE
WESTBOUND
●

CONTENTS

Preface   11

I.

Breakfast with Nuns   15
Remembering Whom I Was Named For   17
Old Photograph   18
Remembering Grandma Lines   19
The Tree   21
Remembering Billy   22
San Antonio Rooming House   23
Mirror   24
My Dying Mother-in-Law   26
Household at 253 Elm Street   28
Promises   29
Firefly   30
Redecorating Nancy's Room   32

II.

To Market, To Market   37
Love Story   38
Ailing   39
October   41
Potato Chips   42
Penmanship   43
Endangered Species   44
Who Listens?   45
Circadian Inquiry   47
His Illness   48
My Husband   49
Watching a Hot Air Balloon   50
Day One After Burial   52
Postmortem   53
Widow   54
I Have Used Up All the Words   55
Now Are We Here   57

PREFACE

Once upon a time there were many hoboes
riding the rails across America.
I remember a few of them
stopping at our house
for a cup of coffee and a slice of bread.
And then the trains disappeared.
And the hoboes disappeared.
Today, only a few are left,
with memories of a westbound that took them to faraway places.

Today's survivors
wait out their twilight years
for the westbound that will take them
to the farthest reaches yet.

These poems celebrate
the waiting for the westbound
by all of us.

I

Remembering

BREAKFAST WITH NUNS

I eat breakfast every morning
with a bevy of nuns long dead,
their shrouds of habits
crumbled to dust somewhere by time
forgetting who they were.
At a flea market
I bought my white antique bowl
nuns once bowed heads over,
prayed over, chuckled over
in maverick moments of escaping frivolity
in the dim hours before dawn,
matins have been mumbled through
to reach the refectory,
preface pause before unwinding
their daily skeins of prayers, play and solitude.
My bowl with logo outlived them all.
I am blessed each morning
eating the body of hopeful saints
who arrowed toward outer space over rosaries
and white breakfast bowls
long before astral investigation
was a government agenda
thinking the fantasy might work.
My bowl remains ghost haunted
humming quietly with Gregorian chants
and female voices muffled
under draped wool hiding hair and cheek,
decades of soap scrubbing a useless abrasive

against my palm-cradled porcelain bowl
the vanished nuns impregnated with themselves.
What we touch remains in place forever,
layer upon layer of skeins of our spent lives
forever increasing earth's girth
with our offerings.

REMEMBERING WHOM I WAS NAMED FOR

Her broken ankle was never set properly
so she limped the rest of her life
asking a cane for assistance.
Going to Swede church
she took the alley
avoiding the sloped front walk
where parishioners with good ankles clotted
and exuberant youths darted helter-skelter like
water bugs, for to impede anyone
was a lack of grace,
nor did she relish pity
a decade old on silver tongues
and averted eyes.
She took the church's back door
and a discreet pew,
closed her eyes to better hear
the *a cappella* of belfry doves
whose muted tremolo was her private introit,
listened to the sermon
sweet Swedish tongued,
nodded at the pulpit promises
confirming her secret tenets.
Her cup of thanksgiving spilled over.
Then she stood on her crooked ankle,
adjusted her shawl,
woke her cane
and limped home
down the alley
alone.

OLD PHOTOGRAPH

I will preserve this face of mine, he said,
and my wife's
and our three sons'
even Shep's
    so they drove into town
    in pressed serge and Sunday silk on Saturday.
Hair smoothed
throats cleared
shoulders squared
pulses throbbing
they stood stone-faced
on a sheepskin rug
waiting for the exploding light
that made a sepia duplicate of them halted in time
in a stance they never took before or after.
    It was night when they reached home
    and unharnessed the horses.
When they unwrapped themselves
covered in glass
and framed in gold
they hung themselves over the organ,
five lives and a faithful dog held in the hands,
their identities preserved forever.

The browsers who found them in the antique shop
wondered who they were.

REMEMBERING GRANDMA LINES

When she was doing it
I never wondered how she did it,
who at eight does?
Now that she claims a weedy plot
surely sunk six inches
in the country cemetery
I could no longer find
had not the mind
the trick of bypassing roads
to arrive suddenly at destinations . . .
now I wonder,
lonesome to ask her face to face.
Widowed at thirty
by typhoid lurking in the well
(and surely the crusty acres
birthing straggly corn rows
and anemic hogs
gave typhoid a hand).
Six children
tugging at her hems and breast,
the swaybacked horse,
the dust pecking chickens,
the meowing barn cats,
the fields begging plowing,
the sun baked garden
crammed with beets, beans and weeds,
ritual investment against hunger,
the hired man bringing his chopped finger
to her to attach with quilt thread,
all these were parasites

sucking sustenance from her
year after year.
But she was stubborn,
wading hobbled through them
the way she waded the creek in August
hunting for black berries.
Her laughter was a musical scale
that plugged up the holes in the house.
Surely out of sight she cried.
There were monthly trips to town to trade,
maybe she pretended the ten miles
would extend to ten thousand
where ice fields and blue chasms
or sandy beaches and palm trees
would swallow up the runaway
and turn her into a pulseless landscape
of her choosing.
Burying one child
and marrying off the others
in happy succession
like a prayer wheel spinning
spun her into a rocker by the window.
A wedding ring quilt in her lap finally finished
was a joyous poultice
over countless cuts and bruises
clumped in the fist
like ravellings.
Forty years too late
I hunger to comfort
this woman, my Grandma Lines.

THE TREE

They cut it down in its prime,
storm damaged, it was necessary,
leaving a gap in the landscape that shocked.
We cringed at the change, the loss,
that mighty metaphor
of sturdy limbs and tousled leaves,
bird residents scattering to flee the chainsaw.
Hypnotized, watching the destruction of the tree
we watched ourselves as well,
our falling foretold,
a bare spot in the landscape,
we hope,
vanity always with us.

REMEMBERING BILLY

We used to laugh loud at you, Billy,
retarded Billy,
You spoke in grunts
often stumbled
couldn't learn,
no special education then.
Sweet, sour, bumpkin, bright,
we were all in the grade school pot together
catching laughter from one another
like chicken pox,
writing on the blackboard
in squeaky harmony,
racing in and out
of raucous recesses,
milk and crackers on our faces.
Did it hurt you, Billy,
retarded Billy,
being laughed at every day?
It hurts me now
years later
remembering.
I'm sorry, Billy.
Can you hear me, Billy?

SAN ANTONIO ROOMING HOUSE

War was an ugly fact
beyond both oceans
but in backtracking the pages
I remember most
the rooming house next door
with the big front porch
and the swing and the creaky rockers
the chummy owners and their tenants
sat in, laughing
at jokes and nickel observations
as each noisy day unraveled:
Planes practicing overhead
in swallow swoops,
Monday night's blackout,
ration books on every kitchen shelf,
the list of dead and wounded on the front page
preceding society's charity ball—
all these were the pile of hickory,
the apple, the sassafras kindling
sturdy on the fireplace floor
holding at its heart
the hurtling hot flames
the cold crowded around
hands extended . . .
even atheists prayed something . . .
The leaping laughter on the front porch
of the San Antonio rooming house
was everybody's incense
tossed on the flames
to sweeten them.

MIRROR

We removed the mirror
to hang wallpaper.
Habit kept turning our faces
to the mirror that wasn't there.
A blank wall
replaced eyes, nose,
mouth, hair,
sometimes teeth
clenched in narcissistic pose
wondering about the dentist next week
    and his drill.
Each gazer was a twin to the other
flesh flesh
glass flesh
same egg origin
the mirror our umbilical cord
with limited length.
We were a comfortable twosome
each departure a painless severing
each returning a spontaneous uniting
a repeated confirmation of our reality.
The mirror gone
we no longer exist
we cannot see who we are
we only guess.
We are lonesome for ourselves
the mirror daily proving
that we *were*
as long as we looked across two feet of space
and smiled at ourselves.

The blank wall
reports nothing but blankness.
Without mirrors
we have only one another
to reflect who we might be.

MY DYING MOTHER-IN-LAW

Wheezing,
flat on your back,
a beside table full of pills—
a ploy by white capped nurses
to seem to outwit your hovering death—
you are sharp as tacks
ten minutes out of every hour.
"Where's Danny?" you ask,
your grandson an affectionate focal point.
"What's he doing in Toledo?"
Then you are gone,
asking about Aunt Annie
who died sixty years ago.

Which body are you in
when you retreat to yesterday,
the new bride's firm pink flesh
or the crumpled parchment skin
you have not seen mirrored for months?
Does your mind give birth in seconds
what connubial consumation exacts almost a year?

Back from your sixty-year glide
I tell you Hilda Hoffman
is moving to a mobile home.
"She won't like it," you say,
"Will she take her cat?"
You cough so violently
a nurse comes running

uncorks a bottle of pink liquid
you shove away
your gown front soggy pink with stubborn rejections.
I tell you good-bye with no response
for you are gone again.
You retire so far this time
they call me next morning to tell me you are dead.

HOUSEHOLD AT 253 ELM STREET

What we have here
is a household of poets
dispensing their wares
from the same podium
at the same time
without conflict,
the haiku of me,
the sonnet of you,
and the free verse of our children
a triumphant trilogy
in spite of erasures
lines cut
words shifted and sifted
waste basket discards
and new beginnings by the thousands
stapled over old endings.

PROMISES

I will not duplicate a thing said
God
and kept His word.
It is man who duplicates
stacks of like after like
clone clogging the universe,
stacks reaching skyward
wobbling sometimes
and tumbling.
But duplication goes on and on
relentless as blood flow
within us.
Is man here
to do what
God
would not,
each faithful to his promise?

FIREFLY

Their quick burst of light
that staccato the summer night
mirror us all.
    Our form shines for a golden moment in the dark . . .
a gift ?   from whom ?
for whom ?
and why ?
    Our form a surprise,
a getting used to,
a blissful marriage of halted time and eternity
in a firefly package . . .
form sees itself
and other forms acknowledge it,
conviction of form assured
by possession of laughter and hunger pains,
even tears wrenched from the blankness of bewilderment.
    We are all small golden suns
pinpricking positions in the universe
for the length of a breath.
for whom ?
and why ?
And then . . .
form vanishes
fast as the firefly trail,
night blankets form,
form that was and form that isn't,
respected objections to leaving rejected

to keep a balance
no human eye has ever measured,
no key has ever unlocked.
Man, with the firefly long tenure
behold yourself on a summer night.

REDECORATING NANCY'S ROOM

Removing the old wallpaper
from your room
was a dry plunge
into memories
pressed flat by time,
sweet scent long gone,
shredded remembrance exiting
to make an imagined improvement
time will surely validate.
One tear of paper and I hear you giggle,
hear that friend—what was her name?
the one with the flame-red hair and braces—
ecstatic with you over Elvis.
Another tear
and you sob with the weight
of geometry
and graduating
and first love gone awry.
I did not know until today
wallpaper cried
and laughed
and became a monk
in a weighted habit
cradling phantom possessions
in empty arms.
The new wallpaper and I
do not know each other.
I resent the intrusion
of this invited guest
brash from the beginning,

waiting for the paste to cool
and the sterile white perfume
to dissipate
heralding acceptance
and a sigh eventually
of redecorating well done.
Come home and see it.
Your self is gone this day.

No one told me
a daughter and her bedroom wallpaper
are bonded for life.
Each new designer's mantle
an imposter . . .
an eraser of poses . . .
a poultice
over old aches and laughter
that eddy away
from the refurbishing stone thrown
into the empty room,
finally to disappear,
the shoreline of walls
weeping good-bye.

II

The Westbound

TO MARKET, TO MARKET

There's a man I buy fish from regularly.
   Across the counter for years
   we have exchanged turbot and money,
   our hands touching briefly like hungry lovers,
   I satisfying my stomach's greed,
   he his rent and cigarette needs.
   We have been in harmony
   without even trying
   except for the expenditure
   of being in place
   on one cubit of the face of earth
   faithfully.

I think dying
   is like buying fish week after week
   from the same man.
   There comes the need to shift performers
   and performances.
   The market place goes on forever,
   other keep jostling and craning their necks
   to discover what our fish and money ritual meant:
   that the world is held in place for the most part
   by such unannotated events
   as being in the same place faithfully day after day.

LOVE STORY

All his teeth were gone,
his grinning at her showed it,
she chuckled, said a sentence,
he nodded, "I knowed it!"
to something she unravelled
from memory and need.
Down the dark alley headed home
they bent together
two hunchbacks with silver hair
pushing a grocery cart
filled with cabbage, noodles,
tuna and Metamucil,
the Social Security exchange doled out
behind them at the supermarket.
They were finishing another night before bed,
their twilight laughter a patch of violets
under the street light,
as they celebrated together
with chuckles and a grocery cart
their holding back once more
each other's final dawn.

AILING

I know a man
who watches fifteen hours
of uninterrupted television each day
except for hobbles
to the bathroom and the fridge.
Emphysema
keeps him chained to a chair
the oxygen tank beside him
his spare pair of lungs
faithful as a nanny.
Not many people
sit cozy beside
their duplicate organs.
He is aware of his uniqueness.
He deserves television,
it is his cherry cobbler reward
for all the bowls of insipid soup.
A ritual kiss on his wife's cheek each morning
and she leaves for work
to buy his air
and cable rent,
their dual duty of going and staying
a situation accepted years ago
without bickering or bartering,
the way stones tumble down a cliff
obeying destiny.
Alone
he enters the picture frame
six feet beyond the soles of his feet,

is sucked a thousand miles away.
He swims
he dives
he hang glides
he digs up old bones
he dances
he lectures
he makes love
he makes deals
he fries catfish,
he is a pauper
he is a prince
he is old
he is young
he is not himself
until he turns off the dial
fifteen hours later,
his out of body travel
ending with a weary jolt.
The television stays warm
behind him, waiting,
waiting for tomorrow.
Tomorrow will come,
won't it?

OCTOBER

One by one
ten by ten
the leaves fall
gilding October.
No window frame escapes
the silent passage
the letting go of tree limb
the graceful glissade,
the arabesque farewell,
the sigh,
the sadness,
the regret
summer is ending.
These mirror my friends,
myself, limb-clinger,
summer beggar.
The obituary page this week
received the fall
of two of my friends.

POTATO CHIPS

His heart fluttered
in that frightening pattern
medicine did not always correct.
His arthritic bones ached.
My own bones were not their best that day.
The gray damp, I guessed,
preferring that crutch of rain drops to bone honesty.
Let's sit a while, he said,
his grin band-aiding uncertainty
flaky as chalk dust.
We nibbled scraps of potato chips
smudging our plates
and toyed with the handles of our coffee cups
waiting for our internal rhythms
to get back into sync
so we could return to the afternoon,
looking across the table at each other
all the while with love
and saying another good-bye
a year already into silent bloom.
Six squirming, squealing youngsters near us
ordered burgers and chips,
blind to us sitting there
growing old
with hidden aches and rusty joints,
hard earned wisdom tucked away,
and monumental love.
Us, mirror of themselves
after their giggles stop.

PENMANSHIP

It was strange.
Approaching death
his script grew small as ant tracks,
a magnifying glass almost needed.
Gone was the robust scrawl
his partner pen humming along
enjoying check buying
or a legal paper finalized.
His name had weight once,
now hospital charts kept track of who he was.
Did his heart,
his lungs,
his glands,
his veins,
his bones,
shrink along with his penmanship?
Instruments in a symphony
share equal responsibility for a cheered finale.
The nurses never shared with me
this creeping incipience
the white sheets cocooned
like metamorphic wrappings.
They just smiled
and kept a secret
I already knew.

ENDANGERED SPECIES

I think
in all the hidden rooms,
the cramped hall space,
the nursing homes,
the old ache most
remembering who they were
when limbs
and lives
and loves ran supple.
Stagnation is seldom borne with grace,
shredded dignity takes its place,
or vapid stare
since being who no one remembers
engenders silence.
The slippered sect is legion, alas.
I pass them quickly
sadly wishing their pantomime
had a solution with laughter in it.

WHO LISTENS?

Who listens when I pray?
God has always been too large,
saints too small,
too mortal,
in spite of numinous acclaim.
Grandma Barkley was called a saint
at Wharton's Bluff.
She baked beautiful bread,
used an outhouse,
buried five sons and two husbands,
and lost the end of her middle finger.
I saw no hovering halo in her eighty-third year,
nor the following year they buried her.
Maybe grief head-on
or mutilated fingers makes saints,
but someone has to see it
and trumpet the findings.
Not many boast, "I am a saint."
Sainthood seekers are a minority,
the office too demanding,
nomination depends on being a mirror
to those who know how to shout to the right people
what they think they have seen,
with the help of quicksilver
and a few documented deeds,
or the insistent voices of kin and community.
Grandma Barkley and the catalogue of saints
and I
have all stubbed our toes,
muddied our shoes,

broken dishes,
broken promises,
had stomach pains,
fevers and chills,
some lustful longings unfulfilled.

Who listens when I pray?
Myself?
Surely myself,
half a century of sieved conundrums suggests it.
There is a wealth of wisdom in me
along with fool and clown.
Until an alternative to self is found
I'll genuflect to me
my staunchest friend
whose gift has always been
to languish with me
love me
console me
listen
listen
listen with and without judgement,
look forward, backward, laugh, lament.
Who else but myself
shares these tears,
comforts these shoulders with a shawl?

All praying is most effective
if you know the listener.

CIRCADIAN INQUIRY

I can no longer remember
the botanical names of a row of bushes
I planted ten years ago,
nor the names of some old friends
faces mirror clear
but labels blurry,
nor some dates with meanings
once upon a time.

Is there a circadian rhythm to forgetting,
a soothing sedative bottled with a pungent prophecy:
once the body lets go its clutch on labels
wisdom winks that labels were only a convenience
in this land of temporary excursions?

HIS ILLNESS

A nurse used to come daily
and stethoscope his intestines,
the secret sound rousing a smile
as if she heard Bach
rising through the twin tubes.
She penned a note
of the presence of the dungeon music
she was taught to detect
for some supervisor
to be glad for confirmation
the body in Room 324 still sang
even though the tune wobbled . . .
was weakening in the *forte* bars.
The hospital housed
a patrolling regiment of nurses,
a stethoscope draped about each neck
like emblems of a holy order
used for listening and recording
the assorted cadenzas
of visiting intestines.

MY HUSBAND

I love you
he said, his body wracked with pain . . .
bent, organs failing,
eyes dimming,
hands trembling,
voice shaking.
I love you
were the same spring flowers
he gave me on our wedding night.
Now they bloomed
from his body's decaying shards,
apart,
vigorous,
perfume unchanged,
the container of no consequence . . .
it still spoke
the abiding symbol,
the majestic myth.
Never was immortality more certain.

WATCHING A HOT AIR BALLOON

Your death
was like a landing hot air balloon collapsing,
slowly,
silent,
stunning,
a Swan Lake performance
surrendering the air
that filled the preened pear hollow
now tumbling
a Greek god in disguise
to die prostrate against the earth.
The balloon's last sigh was ecstasy.
Yours, too, two years ago
but then it seemed a ratchet
faltering, straining to keep the symmetry
of all our yesterdays in place.
The sound wrenched both of us,
words of repair beyond us.
We breathed upon each other,
I on your cheek
you on the sheet that crushed your lungs.
We fought the collapse
but suddenly it was finished.
There was no beauty in the event,
your obituary made no mention of tears,
grief, or the mystery of air in the lungs
transferring allegiance.

Strange . . .
today I watch a hot air balloon collapsing,
bite my lip
and think of you . . .
the beauty of your passing.

DAY ONE AFTER BURIAL

Already rain falls on you
tiptoeing like an intruder.
Yesterday the sun shone warm

as we lowered your casket
toward earth's center,
using careful movements

as if breakage were feared,
sun's glow not dredging our
grief-stricken hearts

but warm on our backs
like some wholesome promise
if we turned in that direction

with Biblical conviction
of rewarded faithfulness.
Today the rain seeps through

the ground toward you.
My mind's ears hear it tunnelling,
begging entrance,

condition the vault seller promised
his product would negate. Strange
how we try to preserve

in sundry ways all that is gone,
you included, knowing better
despite our semantic charades.

POSTMORTEM

I burned stick of incense,
slim and brown as a cattail and made in Tibet.
I did Louis Rukeyser Friday night.
I potted a geranium
replacing a red one that died.
I shuffled through loose photographs
never albumed.
I played a tape with numinous gongs.
I baked a loaf of bread
that finished lopsided.
I bought a new blue blouse.
I ate at the Muffin Shoppe.
None of these worked.
I still miss you.

WIDOW

I miss most the sharing.
I have never seen
a rose split in half
that survives beyond hours.
No matter on which side
the heart lies
blood slows,
the mind leaves footprints
behind itself
solution searching,
no elixir yet
in any cauldron
to offer survival sips
negating withering.
Sepulchral silence
is the warmest wrap I have now.

I HAVE USED UP ALL THE WORDS

I have used up all the words.
No words are left.
Early words served their purpose,
flickering candle flames
lighting the dark a hand span wide,
the gong of early words
a shy tremolo the breadth of an acorn.
I did not know the world's measurements . . .
my vanity lied to me.

Now I need sun words
thunder words
lightening words
words galaxies wide.
There are none.
A beach does not frighten one grain of sand,
awe is the attribute,
the imbalance honored.

I have used up all the words.
I know now
why old folks sit silent.
They have used up all the words,
skeins of connections are cut,
frayed to the breaking point
by the rubbing together of years.
No words are left them.
One talks with death in silence.

NOW ARE WE HERE

"Nu är vi här,"
my grandfather used to say
sitting in his rocker
his beard trembling under the force
of his own maxim
and the recollection of the dotted line
he travelled from Sweden to Illinois.
It meant nothing to me,
sheer prattle,
I was learning to play jacks
embroider lazy daisies
and do the Charleston.

But now I am my grandfather
holding my husband's hand,
feeling it slowly slip from mine,
our journeys arrowing toward a split timetable.
So let us boast aloud with laughter
our conquering the dark
an inch at a time:

Now are we here!

RUTH ALLISON COATES

The poet was born in Mt. Carmel, Illinois on May 18, 1915. She holds degrees from Bethel Women's College, Hopkinsville, Kentucky, and Indiana University. She grew up in a "newspaper household" in Mt. Carmel, and sold her first story at age 15. Her short stories and poems have appeared in publications ranging from *Phylon, Minnesota Review, The Sun,* and *Byline,* to *Guideposts, Parents Magazine* and *Boy's Life.* She is the author of *Great American Naturalists,* published in 1974. Her husband was Robert Coates, an Indianapolis attorney, with whom she raised four children. She was widowed in 1987. Ruth Allison Coates is a member of the Poets Society of America and continues to live and write in Indianapolis and Santa Fe.

Waiting for the Westbound was typeset in Stempel Schneidler and printed on 55-pound Glatfelter Natural at McNaughton & Gunn Lithographers in Saline, Michigan. In the first edition of 1,250 copies, two hundred and fifty are numbered and signed by the author.